CULTURE
SHOCK

Daryl McCann & Debbie Forbes

Promotion of this title has been assisted by
the South Australian Government through the
Department for the Arts and Cultural Development

Omnibus Books,
52 Fullarton Road, Norwood, South Australia 5067,
part of the ASHTON SCHOLASTIC GROUP
Sydney · Auckland · New York · Toronto · London

First published 1995

Copyright © Daryl McCann & Debbie Forbes 1995

Typeset by Clinton Ellicott, Adelaide
Made and printed in Australia by Australian Print Group,
Maryborough, Victoria

All rights reserved

National Library of Australia Cataloguing-in-Publication entry
McCann, Daryl, 1957–   .
Culture shock.
ISBN 1 86291 263 7.
1. Forbes, Debbie, 1959–   . I. Title.

A823.3

Cover artwork by Adam Moyle

For Fran, Don, Eugene and Margaret

and with thanks to Lisa Hood, Ron Pippett,
Charlotte Knottenbelt and Matthew Simpson

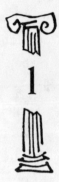

Maybe he shouldn't have done it. The whole thing was only meant as a laugh, but if people were going to make such a big deal about one tiny joke, perhaps he shouldn't have bothered. After all, not everybody's got a good sense of humour, have they?

Michael Sparrow tossed his note from the principal in the nearest bin. Its contents, a request to explain the Tim Vanda incident before school tomorrow, were now firmly lodged in his brain. Besides, if he took the note home he might leave it where his mum might 'accidentally' find it. If there was trouble ahead, better to keep both his mum and dad in the dark for as long as possible.

Forget it, just forget it, Mick told himself, throwing on his footy gear. Trying to leave his worries behind him, he almost sprinted over to the weights room. No one was there, so he decided to fill out the self-assessment chart before the others arrived.

Every week you had to rate yourself according to a number from one to five. A one represented 'pathetic, a mongrel of a game' while at the other end of the scale a five meant 'superb, optimum effort and performance'.

Still only a year ten, Mick had been selected in the First Eighteens a fortnight ago. In each of his two appearances he'd shown flashes of brilliance. He knew it, the coach knew it, and the spectators knew it, but no way was he going to give himself a five. Although his ego was as large and brash as the continent he lived on, Mick had enough sense to hide it from the rest of the team.

After some hesitation he scribbled out a three: 'solid

achievement, good teamwork'. Yeah, that sounded all right, he thought, not too boastful, not too modest.

In any case, his brilliance was acknowledged ten minutes later when the coach called the Firsts together before moving onto the oval. Simon Lupton was science master, but everyone knew his real passion at St Andrews was coaching the First Eighteen. Like each and every individual in the room, he loved his football.

'Okay guys, tell me about Saturday.'

'Good first half. Piss poor after that,' responded Brad Wendt, the captain.

'He's right,' said Mark Pomeroy. 'They're bottom and we only got out of jail at the end thanks to Mick's goal.'

'Top goal!' Jason Ogilvie called out.

'Top goal,' a number of others echoed.

'Yeah, not bad,' agreed the coach, in his usual understated way.

While not showing anything on the surface, Mick felt great. Becoming an accepted member of the Firsts during these past two weeks had to be his best experience ever. He liked everything about it, from the new mates he'd made to the footy fans around the school who now treated him with respect, even if they were older.

Could life get any better than this? It certainly could. The day an AFL team signed him, say in two or three years' time, that's when things would really hot up.

Who was the lucky club going to be? The Crows? Port Adelaide? Quite possibly, but what about the Brisbane Bears? Life on the Gold Coast wouldn't be bad. Then there was the tradition of a Victorian team to consider.

It was at this moment that the unwelcome image of Tim Vanda crept back into his thoughts. A definite uneasiness settled on Mick as he looked over the rest of the team. Might all this, the biggest step forward in his career so far, be taken away from him on account of one small prank?

Out on the oval, the sky was a dull, dirty grey, and a strong, icy wind seemed to blow the team along. Cold in their shorts and guernseys, with Lupton yelling at them and the rain spitting on them, they drudged on through their training. Putting everything into the drills helped Mick forget about tomorrow's meeting with the principal. Anyway, he was enjoying himself.

'This is murder,' complained Jason Ogilvie, taking a breather.

'You're not fit, Jase,' teased Mick. 'Winners thrive on pressure. And let's face it, your body needs a good work-out.'

'Yeah, thanks,' he replied sarcastically.

'Come on, just enjoy it.'

'It's raining, it's freezing,' Jason puffed, hands on hips. 'This wind's straight off the South Pole. It's a crappy day, mate, and it couldn't be worse. Stop being so frigging cheerful, all right?'

Mick just laughed. 'Hey, there's the fan club.' He nodded towards three lunatic year nine girls who were huddled in the score box, watching them train. 'What more could you want?'

'*Your* fan club,' Jason corrected, without a trace of jealousy. 'My own would be nice.'

'They're here for the team, Jase,' Mick assured him, as he sprinted away. However, he did suspect that if he

5

missed a training those girls would soon drift back to the boarding house and not hang around freezing their knees off.

Passing the score box again, Mick noticed his English teacher, Ms Tsouris, watching him thoughtfully as she walked towards the administration block. Probably thinking about pressuring him to join her stupid Culture Club again. Boy she made him mad. 'There're no boys in the club,' she'd said. 'You'd set a good example.'

Of course there were no boys in the club – they had far too much sense to want to go traipsing round bloody art galleries and museums in their spare time. Then she'd started going on and on about his grades and how they could do with improvement.

Damn, he'd bet she was thinking that she hadn't received his assignment! He'd barely started, and it was supposed to be handed in yesterday. Mick gave her a wave, hoping to keep in her good books. If he finished it tonight and crawled a bit tomorrow, maybe he wouldn't lose any marks.

Last night India Seidel got a phone call from Jason Ogilvie, boarder at St Andrews and wingman for the Firsts, inviting her on a second date. She hadn't said yes and she hadn't said no, but instead told him to meet her behind the aviary before school at eight o'clock sharp, by himself and without telling any of his friends.

What had he been thinking of, asking for a second

date? It wasn't as if the first date had been a great success. From the start she knew Jason had no idea where she was coming from. She'd got the impression he misunderstood nearly everything she said, laughing when she hadn't been joking, looking seriously thoughtful when she had.

And it wasn't as if he'd fancied her in the first place. Her mother knew his mother and they'd fixed them up so India wouldn't have to go to the Tregenza wedding on her own.

But if India Seidel knew she wasn't the sort of girl Jason would normally give a second look to, let alone invite out, at some time during the reception at the Hilton she sensed him beginning to enjoy her company. She put that down to his third glass of champagne.

By the time he dropped her off home, he was looking at her as if he thought she was okay, although kissing him goodnight was like kissing a dead fish. The evening had not been a complete failure, but it was hardly the stuff romance is made of, so why the second date offer?

India Seidel was pretty sure she rated very low with

Jason's mates, if she rated at all, not being any kind of football groupie. She knew the type of girls they liked – girls who worked hard at looking sexy, not an easy thing to do in school uniform, with your hair scraped back and no make-up and regulation-length hems. But they did it by giggling and wiggling and looking through their eyelashes.

She figured Jason was just the kind of insecure jerk to worry a lot what his mates thought, and he wouldn't want to be seen with a girl like her, who was known as a loudmouth. So why not ring up some quiet girl with more lip gloss than personality? Must have been his olds pressuring him to take her out again, she decided.

Just how long was the guy going to take? India kicked at the school bag at her feet and stared at the imprisoned cockatoos.

She heard his footsteps and turned around. Good God, he looked keen, even eager. That was all she needed. She tucked a stray red curl back into her ponytail and kept her face serious. 'You tell anyone?'

'Nup,' he smiled.

'Sure?'

He gave her a funny look. 'Of course I'm sure.'

'Ah, that's good,' she said, getting straight to the point. 'Look, about your call.'

'Yeah?' He looked a bit nervous now.

'I wanted to tell you in person. It's only fair. The thing is, I don't want to go out again. Let's face it, we both got pressured into Saturday night. Okay, we've done the right thing by our oldies, so let's just leave it at that. No point carrying on the charade any further, is there?'

'I guess not,' he muttered. She could see he felt hurt.

For the first time India smiled, and tried to make it a bit easier on him. 'You know, I don't know what my mum will come up with next. Parents can be such a pain.'

'Yeah,' agreed Jason, nodding his head.

'I suppose we've just got to be patient with them and hope they don't embarrass us too often,' she grinned.

'Yeah,' said Jason, looking like he wanted to say something back but was somehow unable to think of anything.

Brad Wendt's voice rang out behind them. 'Well, well, look who's lurking around here! I thought it must have been year eights sneaking a cigarette.'

'Hi, Brad.'

'Who's your friend, Jase?'

Jason turned to introduce India, but she was gone.

'Before we go any further,' said Morris Bartel, 'can I assume you're the person responsible for the smoke bomb in Tim Vanda's locker?'

Mick was still feeling slightly unnerved sitting here in the principal's office. Even so, without any hesitation he pushed his blond fringe back from his eyes and confessed. No way was he going to worm out of this. It was all his idea – the other guys were only along for the laugh. More than anything else, Mick Sparrow prided himself on his honesty and his ability to face things head-on.

'What was the bomb made of? So far we've only recovered some aluminium foil.'

Mick didn't like sharing such secrets, but he wasn't

going to dodge any of the principal's questions either.

'Wrap a ping-pong ball in foil and ignite the ball, then cover it up straightaway. The ball disintegrates almost instantly. Guaranteed to cause more smoke than a house on fire,' said Mick, managing not to smile while recalling the look on Vanda's face when he thought his locker was on fire. 'But there's no danger of anything catching alight.'

The principal thumped his fist on the table. 'The whole damned corridor was filled with smoke! You realise we nearly had the fire brigade in?'

'It was just a joke, that's all.'

Bartel leaned forward in his chair. His teeth were showing but his eyes were cold. 'It's true, isn't it, that a victory against a top team like Sacred Heart this week would mean we're starting to get somewhere?'

'Something like that,' responded Mick. He knew, knew all along, St Andrews would use the one thing he actually liked about the place against him. This college was so predictable.

'What a tragedy, then, if one of our newest and most talented members were unavailable for the game.'

12

Mick was now looking at the carpet, waiting for Bartel's twist of the knife.

'Let me make it clear to you, lad, so there's no mis-understanding. You're in serious strife, and it's not just the smoke bomb business. We now know you've been harassing Tim Vanda for over two years. Punching him on the oval last year, threatening him on the way home, victimising him in the school yard, hiding his textbooks and folders, and attaching an "I'm gay" sticker to the back of his blazer in science.'

Mick looked up, almost shocked. Of course he'd occasionally hassled the guy, but it had only ever been done as a laugh. The principal made it sound worse than it was, as if Mick was some kind of bastard obsessed with humiliating Vanda at every opportunity.

The picture Bartel was drawing didn't fit with the one Mick had of himself. It made him seem nasty, even cruel, and Mick – along with a lot of other people – knew he wasn't like that.

He was also surprised that Vanda had done such a thorough job. Over the years the guy had never once dobbed him in, and yet now he'd gone and tipped the whole bloody bucket over him. He'd sure picked a good time.

'I think we need the sort of punishment that fits the crime,' announced the principal.

Mick rubbed his chin as he weighed up the chances of playing another game for the Firsts this season. Not very likely, he concluded, not very likely at all.

The principal's voice continued on. 'A week of lunch-time bucket duty for starters.'

Mick nodded. He'd pick up papers for the rest of the year as long as his football career wasn't messed up.

'Now as far as the First Eighteen is concerned ...'

Despite his intention to tough it out and face things head-on, he looked at the principal with pleading eyes: like a hungry dog pleading for a bone, Mick later reflected.

Bartel paused as he sat back comfortably in his chair. He had this Michael Sparrow right where he wanted him.

'Now,' said the principal, smiling. 'I wonder if we might come to some kind of arrangement ...'

Mick nodded.

'Do you know how the Culture Club works?' Bartel asked.

Mick didn't, but had the sinking sensation he was about to find out.

India was late, thanks to her little brother and his tantrums. She slammed the car door then marched off towards the bus, feeling happier with every step. It was great to get away from Oscar the Terrible and have a nice night out. She looked hard at the girls getting on the bus, trying to pick out Vanessa Chan, her best friend.

There she was, talking to Mick Sparrow. Mick Sparrow, that turkey! She'd forgotten he'd come to the last club meeting. What was *he* doing on an excursion? The guy really made her blood boil. He was such a football hero, you wouldn't think he'd have to join a club like this to pick up his next girlfriend. It wasn't as if he had any kind of brain to bring to a cultural gathering.

Seeing India, Vanessa said goodbye to Mick and went over to her friend. Together they chose a seat near the front of the bus and started talking with the other girls in loud, cheerful voices.

Mick, meanwhile, sat down near the back by himself and stared gloomily at his reflection. He was beginning to feel a bit lonely and depressed, not to mention annoyed.

A waste of an evening, that's what he called it. Some one-man show by a guy called Jim Maddison. He could have been doing his science project or watching TV or listening to his latest CD or just about anything.

He had to admit, though, his first Culture Club meeting at lunch-time hadn't been too bad, with everyone being pretty friendly, except that grumpy India girl. Vanessa had been good to talk to as they waited for the bus to come, and though none of the girls had come to sit with him on the bus, most had said hello and smiled.

When they came to go into the theatre, at least he didn't have to sit by himself. Ms Tsouris called him over to sit next to her, and then some year eleven girls sat on the other side.

Vanessa and India were sitting as far away from Mick as possible. India had seen to that. 'He's so ignorant he'll probably talk all the way through!' she had declared.

Vanessa laughed, 'Yeah, sure. As if Ms Tsouris would let anyone say anything once the show started, especially someone who's sitting next to her.'

'Well, I just don't like him,' said India, feeling she had to explain herself.

'I still don't see what you've got against him,' Vanessa replied. She had enjoyed talking to Mick before. He seemed like a nice guy.

'Footballer,' replied India. 'That one word explains everything.'

'What have you got against footballers?'

18

'Ness, you probably think the word "footballer" just means "someone who plays football", but it also means "thickhead, culturally stupid, egomaniac and sexist pig". Believe me.'

'But you don't even *know* Mick Sparrow,' countered Vanessa. She hated it when India implied she didn't know what an English word meant.

'He's in my humanities class. Besides, footballers are all the same.'

'Oh, yeah?' Vanessa was really angry now. 'The next thing you'll be telling me is that all Chinese are the same! Remember, we all look the same, don't we?'

'I didn't mean that,' India said as the lights were going down for the show to start, but her friend was looking straight ahead, refusing to speak to her. Vanessa didn't lose her temper very often, but when she did, it always took her a long time to get over it.

India just loved Gin Maddison. The woman was a genius! Virginia Maddison had done lots of small parts in famous movies and though she was young and brilliantly talented she just wasn't good-looking enough to ever be the main star. That was one of the things that made India so cross. If you were a man it was okay to be short with a big nose. It certainly hadn't done Dustin Hoffman's career any harm.

She sat down by herself in the bus, no longer worried that Vanessa was still ignoring her, for all she could think of was the marvellous performance. The section called 'Objects' had been very strange, but she liked it. Gin played the part of a pencil to perfection! Then she was a desk lamp, a sliding door and a kettle.

'Like the show?' asked Ms Tsouris, slipping into the seat next to her.

'It was wonderful!' smiled India. 'The scene where she played the two women shopping was so funny.'

'Yes, I thought you'd like it,' the teacher replied. 'But it's not to everyone's taste. The newspaper gave the show a terrible review. Did you read it?'

India was about to give her opinion of theatre journalist Quentin Marshall and his narrow-minded, self-satisfied, childish reviews, when a burble of laughter floated down from the back of the bus.

Turning around India saw Mick, half standing up, holding his nose pressed flat to his face saying in a squeaky voice, 'I'm a pencil! I'm a pencil!' while the girls around him dissolved into laughter. Then he held one arm out to the side and, still squashing his nose, started to sway like a sliding door.

With a start India realised even Ms Tsouris was laughing, and had moved off to sit with him.

This is what she had suspected all along. You couldn't have a guy like Michael Sparrow in a club like this because he would ruin everything. It worried her that no one else could see how dangerous he was. India gritted her teeth in determination: she would have to make them see.

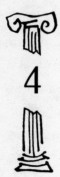

It was a brilliant moment. Mick had been too nervous to have any of his friends there when he looked up this week's First Eighteen against Sacred Heart on the notice board. After last Saturday he hardly expected to be dropped, but neither had he expected a promotion to the half-forward flank. Tomorrow he would be able to attack the goals right from the start of the match instead of only in the final quarter.

A hand tapped him on the shoulder.

Brad Wendt was smiling at him. 'I reckon you might do some real damage from the forward line.'

Mick only hesitated for a second. 'I don't care where they play me, as long as I can contribute to the overall team game. On the day it's the team that matters, not the individual,' he replied.

'Exactly,' said Brad, giving him a friendly punch to the arm.

Mick smiled to himself, happy he could play both the game of football *and* the game of life so well. While he wouldn't have minded staring at that notice board all morning, he left Brad and took off for his locker.

Stepping back down into the undercroft, Mick noticed a girl come into view. She was heading straight for him. What did she want? Although they were in the same humanities class, India Seidel and he didn't get on at all. A lot of girls seemed to enjoy his company, and Mick thought those who didn't were probably just shy.

India was different, because though she avoided him, she certainly wasn't lacking in confidence. In class

23

she gave her opinions on things even when no one asked for them. She always seemed intense and grumpy, criticising everything people said, even when it was Mr Leonard, the humanities teacher. She was … a pain.

'I want to talk to you,' she said.

'Yeah? About what?'

'The Culture Club. I don't know what you were playing at last night, but people don't want you coming along again.'

'Is that so?' He thought he'd been a great success on the bus home, but her bossy tone made him unsure. In normal circumstances, of course, he would have told India Seidel where she could stick her precious club, but there was that deal he'd made with Bartel.

'Yes it is. A person like you doesn't fit in.'

'And why's that?' he demanded to know.

The look in her eyes threw him off balance. She didn't simply dislike him – no, the force of her feelings was much more powerful than that. He could see she actually hated him.

'Because you're a wanker,' she hissed.

He was stunned. Talking to this girl was like having your face slapped. 'Bugger off,' he replied, sounding nothing like his usual confident self. Thank God none of his mates were witnessing this.

'You just make sure you don't turn up for the excursion on Sunday,' she threatened, then tore off.

At first Mick didn't want to admit how much she'd got to him. Then he realised he was walking in the opposite direction to his locker.

'What a bitch,' he muttered.

He stopped to turn back and noticed a woman in the visitors' car park, staring. She seemed familiar. When he saw Tim Vanda in the distance loading books into the back of a car, he knew why.

She walked towards him. 'Tim's leaving today.'

'I didn't know,' Mick said, in the same respectful voice he'd used with her when he was twelve.

'I think it's for the best, but it is a big decision. He really looked forward to coming here. Back in primary school you and Tim were always talking about how great it was going to be at St Andrews.'

'Yeah, I suppose we did.'

Over the years Mick hadn't exactly forgotten about his primary school friendship, but it certainly wasn't a subject he thought much about. Now, though, it almost came as a surprise to recall the amount of time he'd once spent with the Vanda family. Mick had often stayed over their place. It was where he'd learnt to play chess, fly his first kite ... they had even taken him on a holiday to Port Hughes one summer.

The Vandas used to have a dog called Sasha, a black terrier. It got cancer and one afternoon Mr Vanda took it to the vet to be put down. Mick had been there when Tim heard the news. Tim had cried. Jesus! Now he remembered – that day even Mick had cried.

'Tim's going to Glynburn. I just pray things will work out better there.'

'I hear it's a good school,' said Mick.

Mrs Vanda smiled, but her lip was trembling. She looked around at Tim, still hovering by the car. 'You're a cool customer, aren't you?' she said, tears in her eyes.

He didn't get a chance to answer her question, because in an instant she was gone. As Mick watched mother and son drive off, he tried to work out how he'd ever managed to be Tim Vanda's friend.

Mick knew Mr and Mrs Vanda would be blaming him for things going wrong with their son. Of course he had to take some of the blame, but that was still missing the point. You could count the kids who liked Tim Vanda on five fingers – cut off at the knuckles. And his new school would be no different.

Mick groaned, not sure if he was more sorry for Tim or himself. Copping India Seidel and Mrs Vanda all in one go was a bit much. He hadn't checked his horoscope this morning, but it probably said something like 'Beware of critics'.

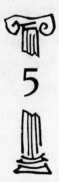

Before each game, Mick liked to keep strictly to the same routine. On Friday night his mum cooked pasta, because it contained lots of carbohydrates, and carbohydrates meant energy. Dinner finished, he watched an hour of television then turned in early, whether there was a good party on or not. Saturday mornings he usually got up at seven and had two pieces of toast, some orange juice and whatever fruit was handy.

After breakfast his dad, Ray, always drove him to Morphettville Racecourse where he did a few loosening up exercises before a circuit of the track.

Years ago Raymond Sparrow had been good enough to play two games of league football before he'd done a cartilage in a motorbike accident. He went through a series of successful operations but there was never any chance of him playing competitive sport again, let alone at league level. If there were to be a famous footballer in the family, it was going to have to be his son.

Mick never pushed himself on his Saturday morning run. It was mainly a chance to concentrate on the game ahead. This morning, however, it took longer than usual to clear his mind of all the unimportant things in life. He found himself clenching his teeth every time he thought of India Seidel. Who the hell did she think she was? And then there was that talk with Mrs Vanda while Tim loaded his school things into the back of the car.

Eventually his mind began to focus properly. One way he achieved this was by thinking about inspirational moments in sport. Probably his favourite was Dean Jones' 210 in Madras, India, even though it

29

happened a long time ago. In 37°C heat and 87 per cent humidity, Jones had batted until he was almost unconscious. In the end he was rushed to hospital, lucky to escape death from dehydration.

From the moment he read that story, Mick understood what had driven Dean Jones on. It wasn't madness, as some experts liked to claim, but that special ingredient in all champions – courage.

After an early lunch, usually hot dogs and mustard, his dad drove him to school. Even if it was an away match, the First Eighteen always gathered at St Andrews first, everyone in their full school uniform.

Mick didn't particularly like wearing a blazer and tie on weekdays, but Saturday before the big game was different. On Saturday it meant something, because it marked you out as the member of an elite. Mick even found himself standing straighter and taller, while all the parents and fans seemed to slouch in their jeans and tracksuits.

As the team headed off for the two-kilometre drive to Sacred Heart, Mick couldn't help remembering that this was the same bus they'd gone in to the Festival

Theatre on Thursday night. He shook his head as he thought about the way Bartel had blackmailed him into joining the Culture Club.

Tomorrow there was another bloody excursion, this time to some art gallery. After today's game there were three matches left in the football season, so that meant he only had to put up with the Culture Club for three more weeks. And that's all it would be – three weeks.

In the dressing room before the match, everyone was in high spirits. And when Simon Lupton, the coach, drew the team in and belted out his message, the atmosphere was electric. Players shouted out encouragement and patted each other on the back. What had Brad Wendt said to him yesterday? 'Mick, I reckon you might do some real damage from the forward line.' All right then, let's do some damage.

By the time he ran on to the Sacred Heart oval he was ready to play the best game in his life. He was greeted by the cheers, applause, boos and car horns of 200 spectators. Not exactly the roar of 48,000 Crows fans, but so what? Mick was pumped up.

His first goal was a gift. At the sixty-second mark of the first quarter the ball came off a pack, and all he had to do was soccer it through from five metres out. He was proud of the second one a few minutes later. He chipped the ball forward to one of his team mates and kept going. Suddenly the ball was back in his hands and, magically finding his balance, he threaded it through the two white posts.

But his best play was still to come. When the ball headed straight back into the St Andrews' forward line, Mick was there. He faked out his opponent and stretched for the ball on a sharp lead. He ran and ran and actually had it safely in his hands when something hard exploded into the side of his head. It was a fist.

The crowd went dead, everything went dead. The only sound he heard was a strange noise in his right ear, like the hum of an old computer. The only thing he saw was the photograph of a girl's face. It was a black-and-white photo, or at least red and white. But whose face was it? And then the girl came alive and suddenly spoke to him.

'I'm not sure about my feelings,' she said.

'You either love me or you don't,' replied Mick. 'It's simple.'

'Feelings are never simple. They're complicated, like they've got a mind of their own. They never seem to do what they're told.'

Mick was angry – he wanted a straight answer. 'We're not talking about a pet dog here, we're talking about love.'

She just laughed, and walked towards her front door without a backward glance.

Mick stood there, devastated.

Then he snapped back into consciousness. Where was he? In the change room at Sacred Heart, that's where.

Bert, the head trainer, came over to dab a wet flannel on Mick's forehead. 'That's the end of the game for you,' he said in his rough voice. 'Bad luck, because you were playing so well.'

'What happened?' asked Mick, trying to sit up on the bench.

'Biffo, young Mick. Someone snotted you good and proper. I hope the umpire got his bloody number.'

Despite the piercing headache, it was a real disappointment to realise his game was over. It was also disappointing, not to mention confusing, to realise that the face of the girl in his dream belonged to none other than India Seidel.

India didn't hate Oscar, her three-year-old brother, but sometimes she didn't exactly like him. All evening he'd been a real terror. To start with he wouldn't eat his dinner, so she'd had to force feed every last noodle into him. Then he started bawling his eyes out, and wouldn't shut up until she bribed him with chocolate, chocolate she'd been keeping for Vanessa and herself. After that he made them watch his latest Walt Disney video all the way through.

When she eventually put him to bed, he kept calling out over the intercom every few minutes for another story. She and Vanessa took it in turns reading him *Jim Goes Shopping*, *The Trouble With Jim*, *Jim's Outing*, *More Trouble With Jim*, *Here Comes Jim*, and *Where's Jim?* until they were both heartily sick of Jim and his adventures.

In desperation, India invented a story of her own, *Jim's Bedtime*. She told that one twenty times, but it wasn't until after nine-thirty that he took the hint. As with most Saturday nights, India's parents were out working in their restaurant. For staying home and babysitting she got paid twenty dollars, but it never seemed nearly enough.

There was another reason why India didn't always appreciate Oscar's presence. Her real father, Tom Seidel, left when India was in year two. He lived in Mount Gambier now and she hardly ever saw him, which suited her just fine. Gail, India's mother, remarried four years ago and Oscar was one of the results. A part of India couldn't help seeing her little brother – along with her stepfather for that matter – as something of an intruder.

'Thank God,' she said, settling back in her beanbag now the intercom had finally gone silent. 'Looking after Oscar is only slightly worse than a date with Jason Ogilvie.'

'Actually, I think he's cute in a gawky sort of way.'

'Oscar?'

'No, Jason.'

India frowned. 'If you keep saying stuff like that, Ness, I'm going to have to terminate our friendship.'

Vanessa laughed, and that made India smile. She knew her friend thought she was sometimes a bit over the top with her opinions. They'd only been friends since last year when they were in the same English class, but Vanessa had seemed to like her personality straightaway.

After a class speech where everybody else had struggled to get past the two-minute mark, and India had done an eight-minute-thirty-second blockbuster on the life and times of Wolfgang Amadeus Mozart, without pausing – not even when some boy in the back row started making snoring noises – Vanessa had come up and told her how great she was. Most kids would have probably thought India was a complete jerk for taking the speech so seriously.

Vanessa was always polite, careful not to offend, while India was completely unworried by what other people thought of her. If she wanted to do something, then watch out anyone who tried to stop her; but if she didn't want to do something nobody in the world – except a screaming Oscar – could make her. This probably explained why, in spite of her intelligence, she rarely got A's in any of her subjects, even music and drama. Whenever an assignment failed to grab her interest, she would either refuse to do it or try to get away with passing it in late.

Her most recent success was the time she promised the science teacher that an overdue term report would be in his pigeon-hole by three-thirty that afternoon. Trouble was, she didn't get around to finishing it by then.

The next morning before school, Vanessa had watched her fold up the assignment a couple of times and push it right to the back of Mr Dragenheim's pigeon-hole. In science, when he asked her where it was, India looked him right in the eyes and, as innocent as anything, said he couldn't have checked his pigeon-hole properly.

In the following lesson Mr Dragenheim actually apologised for his oversight. India was happier about that than if she'd scored an A for the whole year.

Vanessa took a sip of the beer they'd stolen from the drinks fridge in the back laundry. 'Even if footballers *are* a lower form of life, you didn't have to abuse the hell out of Michael Sparrow.'

'Maybe I was a bit rough on him, but he asked for it.'

'How?'

'The Culture Club is ours.'

'But it's for everyone.'

'That's where you're wrong. It's the one place where people like us can really learn without having to jump through all those hoops teachers make for us. I'm sick of their stupid tests and always adding up marks, treating us like we're circus animals. I'm almost sixteen. I can think for myself. I don't want to be tricked or frightened into learning. I want to learn what I want to learn. That's why the Culture Club is what's real at St Andrews, and everything else is false. Most of the time it's like ...' India ran a hand through her hair as she tried to think of the right comparison. 'For God's sake, Ness, it's like being in an expensive day-care centre!'

'I agree, I agree, but don't forget Mick chose to join

the Culture Club. Even if it's part of his strange sense of humour or something, he's still giving up his own time when he comes along.'

India sighed and was silent for a moment. 'I tell you what. If he turns up tomorrow after the mouthful I gave him on Friday, I'll go easier on him.'

'Is that a promise?'

'Hey, don't push it. And stop hogging that beer.'

Stuff the Culture Club, he thought, trying to make sense of the painting in front of him. He'd paid five dollars of his own money to enter this special exhibition wing of the art gallery. The display was entitled 'German Post-Deconstructionist Art' and Mick had hoped it might contain pictures of the First or Second World War or something interesting like that.

What he found instead was a series of the most pathetic drawings he'd seen since his days at Camden Junior Primary School. And that was probably being unfair on the average six-year-old.

Every single painting here, with no exception, was a

piece of crap. They were all just scribbles and circles and splashes of bright paint with no point to them at all. The only good thing was the frames. One dork had even glued pieces of wood over the top of his master-piece. Did somebody really pay to have this garbage flown all the way out from Germany? Mick had a mind to go and see the principal tomorrow. If the principal wanted him to keep coming on outings like this, then the school should start subsidising him.

Mick was depressed enough already when he saw India Seidel approaching. That's all he needed. The whole afternoon he'd been trying to avoid her. He was still feeling groggy from being knocked out, and the last thing he wanted was her ripping into him again.

'Like it?' she asked.

Mick sighed. Of course *she* would like it because she was so bloody pretentious. He was tempted to lie, just to avoid a confrontation, but even concussed he wasn't going to play dead.

'I reckon it sucks,' he answered, defiantly.

'I think you're probably right,' she smiled, and floated off to the other side of the room.

He watched the back of her for a moment, scratching his head. Mick hadn't forgotten yesterday's dream, but now he wished he could. Anyway, things like that didn't mean anything, did they?

He bit his lip.

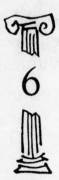

Mick and India stood side by side by the podium on stage in the drama centre, looking at the concert plan she had drawn up. They both felt very uncomfortable about being so close together, but each was determined not to let the other know.

Not for the first time, Mick cursed Ms Tsouris. It was another one of her stupid bright ideas that he work with India to organise a special performance highlighting the school's musical talents. He glanced sideways at his least favourite female, wondering how she was coping with the fact of having to work with him. He could hardly be her first choice – she must be spitting chips. Nah, she looked all calm and business-like. He felt a twinge of disappointment.

'We have to start with the flautists, because they're quiet, and move slowly towards the more noisy instru-ments,' India stated, trying to keep her voice steady. She had been fuming since Ms Tsouris lumped them together on this project, but she was damned if he was going to know she cared.

It was obvious he had the hide of an elephant and the stubbornness of a mule, because after all her abuse he hadn't even missed a single meeting. Look how close he was standing now! Pretending to be interested in the program, but really just trying to piss her off, she'd bet. Maybe she could freeze him off with chilly politeness? 'We'll finish, of course, with the best routines from the school musical. People are always more willing to sit quietly at the beginning, and it's best to finish with the liveliest numbers, so that means ...'

'No way,' interrupted Mick. 'Start with whatever's

second best for noise and action – really hit them with the goods.'

'You're thinking of debating – second best point, worst point, best point,' India said scornfully. 'This is not a debate, it's a mini-concert.'

'Look, I've never done debating,' Mick replied, wondering why he cared what they started with. He'd been going to say okay to the plan, whatever she'd written, and get off home quick smart, but he hadn't liked the way she assumed she could tell him what was going to happen. 'But I have seen the Royal Variety Performance on TV, and they started with a big song-and-dance number this year. It was so good I kept watching through all the boring bits waiting for another one.'

'Okay,' agreed India.

'Okay?' Mick looked at her. He couldn't believe she'd give in so quickly. 'What, no argument?'

'Mick,' she smirked, looking him straight in the eyes, 'if it kept *your* attention, it must be a pretty good way of presenting things. After all, it's the cultural cretins that concern me. I don't want you wrecking things for the rest of us.'

'Cultural cretin? Well, thanks a lot. I'm a member of the Culture Club, aren't I? If I didn't think culture was important, why would I be here?'

'Why indeed? I used to think you were some kind of anti-culture spy, but then I figured a spy needed three qualities.'

'What?' He hated himself for asking.

'Intelligence, principles and acting ability,' smiled India. 'And as you fail miserably on three counts, I guess I'm wrong.'

Mick didn't know what to say. India really got a kick out of putting the boot in: her eyes were sparkling and her cheeks were flushed. It surprised him to notice she looked almost pretty for once. Boy, he wished he could wipe that smug look off her face, but what would that achieve? They were going to be working together for the next three weeks and, while she might be able to get out of it, he'd have to keep showing up.

'Listen,' he sighed. 'We've got a lot to do and not much time to do it in, so if it's all right with you I'd rather we cut the insults and just got on with our work. I mean, this is for all those parents whose kids might be coming here next year, so we'll look pretty stupid if we've spent all our time arguing and the whole show's a shemozzle.'

'Yeah,' agreed India, 'I take your point.' She'd never expected Mick to have such a mature attitude. 'If it's so important, you'd think the school would get a teacher to organise it, not us.'

'Well at least a teacher might give the parents credit for not being cultural cretins,' quipped Mick.

'I thought we weren't having any more insults.'

'Couldn't resist it. Well, what order shall we put the program in then?'

They bent their heads back over the concert plan and focused on the job they had to do, starting a pattern of cooperation that they somehow managed to keep up through the meetings and rehearsals of the next week.

India, peering intently at the small model in the glass

case, didn't realise Vanessa was standing behind her until her friend spoke.

'Isn't this fabulous? Must be the best excursion we've had all year.'

'You're only saying that because we get out of school, and double maths at that,' smiled India.

'Well, that helps,' Vanessa admitted, 'but I never would have thought theatre sets could be so interesting. There's some really high-tech stuff in the auditorium. I'm going to take another look. Have you seen it?'

India hadn't. She'd been absorbed in the models of sets from famous shows of the past. 'Let's go.'

'Can you believe all these year eight boys?' asked Vanessa. 'What on earth's made them join the Culture Club all of a sudden? Maybe they get out of maths too.'

India looked over to the group of small fry gathered around the barricades set from Les Misérables. In the middle of them stood Mick Sparrow, reading aloud from the placard that explained how it worked. 'They're worshipping their hero,' she remarked drily. 'A bunch of sheep, following the leader.'

'You should be glad they've followed him here,' grinned Vanessa, 'instead of on to the football pitch.'

'Oh, I'm sure they've followed him there, too. Let's just hope he doesn't decide to jump off the chapel spire.'

India was fascinated with the exhibition, but her gaze kept wandering over to Mick and his disciples. He looked full of enthusiasm when he spoke to them, as if he was really getting something out of it. 'Yeah,' India thought, 'another ego trip.' But she didn't really mean it. He was starting to get to her. She could feel little buds of respect sprouting on her bad opinion of him, making it into something else.

Suddenly India realised he knew she was watching him. He gave her a wink and she felt her cheeks flush hot pink as she turned away. 'I will not look at him again. I will not look at him again,' she ordered herself. 'God, I'm an idiot!'

But a few moments later her gaze drifted back to him.

Monday's rehearsal after school was their first and last dummy-run for the parents' music exhibition. There was still almost a week to go before the performance, but this was the only day that didn't clash with sport practice.

Mick and India stood together in the wings. Their job for the performance was to act as co-presenters. Ms Tsouris, wearing an intercom headset, was behind the stage, making sure the performers kept quiet and were ready to go on at the right moment, and Vanessa was up in the lighting box, also in a headset, so she could report any onstage hitches to Ms Tsouris.

Over the past few days Mick felt different whenever he had to work with India. They both acted in a business-like way as they spoke to other students about their performances, but they hardly said a word to each other that they didn't have to. It probably looked as if they weren't getting along, but it wasn't that.

He found himself standing or sitting quite close to her when he didn't mean to, and doing strange things like studying the waves in her thick, auburn hair when her back was turned to him, or watching her face closely when she was speaking to someone else.

Here in the wings he stood next to India, waiting for Ms Tsouris to cue them to come on for the introduction. Mick realised again he was much closer to her than he needed to be. Just as he was about to move back, India turned and flashed him a small, quick smile. Did she know what he was going to say? Was she encouraging him?

'Want to come to the Show Thursday night?' he asked.

'With you?'

'Yeah, course with me.'

'I'd rather die of embarrassment. In fact, I probably would.'

'What? Because I'm a footballer? I haven't asked you to a Crows game.'

'You could ask me out to a French restaurant and I wouldn't go. Not even if it was in Paris and you threw in first class Qantas tickets.'

'I was thinking more of a hot dog on the ferris wheel.'

'Sounds appealing!' mocked India. 'But unfortunately it's my turn to wash the dishes on Thursday night.'

Mick was stuck for something to say. He'd thought he was pretty good at asking girls out. He wanted to think of another way to persuade her, but she just didn't seem interested. Perhaps he'd read her wrong; maybe she didn't like him after all.

At that moment he noticed Ms Tsouris frantically waving from the other side of the stage for them to go on. God knows how long she'd been signalling to them.

'Oops, looks like we're on,' said India.

'Yeah,' Mick sighed.

51

'Hey, I'll let you in on a secret,' she whispered urgently. 'But you've got to promise you won't tell anyone.'

'Whatever.'

'Promise.'

'Sure,' he shrugged.

'I just remembered, we've got a dishwasher. Six-thirty and don't be late.'

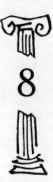

The doorbell rang downstairs. Leaving someone else to answer it, India took another look at herself in the dressing-table mirror.

'Mick's here!' her mother called, but she still didn't rush down. They'd want to give him some kind of interview.

She looked okay, she guessed, but somehow she still wasn't satisfied. They were going to the Royal Show, so there was no point being too dressed up for a night of carnival rides and leaky hot dogs. Jeans and an olive green sweatshirt felt pretty good after a week of school uniform, but for the first time in her life India had a small desire to be glamorous. She quickly added lipstick, then rubbed it off. It might look like she was trying too hard.

Walking slowly down the stairs, she could hear Mick's teasing voice and Oscar whooping with boisterous laughter. 'Little turd,' she thought, 'turning on his charm for a stranger.'

Bending down to look through the banisters and through the open french doors that led in to the lounge room, India could glimpse her stepdad smiling and Mick down on the ground in a rough and tumble fight with Oscar. It annoyed and impressed her at the same time. She knew better than anyone how difficult Oscar was to win over, and Mick had managed it in minutes.

'Hi, Mick, guess we better get going,' India announced, as if they were already running late. The last thing she wanted was to hang around in this over-bright room with the olds watching her watching Mick and Oscar stealing the show.

They were catching the tram. India knew her step-dad would have been happy to take them and pick them up, but it didn't seem like much of a date that way. Mick had ridden to her house, and as they walked across the lawn she noticed his bike chained to the inside of their picket fence with his fluorescent bike helmet on the grass beside it, almost hidden by a daisy bush.

Was it dumb to go on the tram? Someone might see them together. Perhaps going to the Show was a dumb idea too. When Mick asked her, India had been tempted to suggest they go to the movies instead; less chance of being spotted there. But then she figured the Show was dark and crowded and they wouldn't stand out against the thousands of other teenagers. But the tram? That would be light and full of locals. 'Maybe I should have worn a hat and dark glasses,' India muttered to herself as they walked, conversationless, along the pavement.

'What?' asked Mick.

'Nothing, just talking to myself.'

'Not worried about being seen with me, are you?' He

sounded indignant, although the same thought had crossed his own mind.

'No one likes to be the target of the latest gossip.'

'Maybe we should just sit on different seats on the tram and meet by the ferris wheel in half an hour,' sneered Mick. 'Nah, people might see us. How about we meet up in the hall showing the latest farm equipment? No one from school will be looking in there.'

He thought about holding her hand as they got on the tram. That would really piss her off! But *he* didn't really want to look that obvious either. It was funny going on a date with someone you both liked and didn't like. Was that how she felt about him? She must like him a fair bit, he decided, or she wouldn't be here, risking her precious football-hating reputation. It was kind of flattering, really, when you thought of it like that.

There was no one they knew on the tram. Mick seemed pretty cheerful and rattled on for a while, telling India about a new guy at school he'd been sitting next to in maths. The guy's father had spent the last five years working on a Pacific island and the family had had many adventures – some dangerous, some humorous. When he told her about the time the guy had to strip off in public because tropical ants had crawled up his legs, India suddenly realised she was laughing loudly and the people in front of her were glancing round to see where the noise was coming from.

Mick was good fun, she decided, and it would be stupid to spoil their date worrying about what everyone else thought. She'd always hated people who wouldn't do something because it wasn't 'the thing to do', and there she was, almost becoming one of them!

At the Show they bought thickshakes and wandered around the rides, trying to decide which were the best. They'd both been on some of them last year. India drew the line at anything that went upside-down.

'I'm not chucking up chocolate thickshake in public, and that's final,' she insisted.

'Well, I'm not going on the Mad Mouse,' countered Mick. 'I went on that when I was a kid and hated it. The ups and downs were good, but I couldn't stand that feeling every time you went round a corner, that you were going to shoot right over the edge instead.'

57

'Let's start with the Matterhorn,' she said. 'That doesn't look too scary. Then you pick the next ride, and then we could go on that boat thing that flies up in the air really fast. I reckon that's about the worst I can stand.'

They pushed through the crowds to join the queue for the ride. The queue was so long it took fifteen minutes before they got into a little carriage for five minutes of speed that pleasantly squashed them together.

Then they wove through the crowds again to Mick's choice and waited another fifteen minutes. The noise level was tremendous. Every ride pumped out music, everyone was talking and people on the rides were screaming. Mick and India had to keep their heads close together just to hear what they were saying.

After the second ride Mick had had enough.

'Come on,' he said, taking India's hand and pulling her along through the crowds so they wouldn't get split up.

'Where are we going?' she yelled, but he could hardly hear her.

Finally they were in a quieter area, away from the rides and surrounded instead by small buildings and thinner crowds than before.

'I couldn't stand that noise any longer,' said Mick, still holding on to her hand. 'Let's get something to eat, I'm starving.'

They walked together through the back buildings of the Show, with India pulling Mick through the display hall because she wanted to look at the photographs and the decorated cakes. He was going to say it was boring, but she made fun of all the cakes and photographs he considered a waste of time and pointed out some really good ones, so he enjoyed himself without meaning to.

Then they found a Pizza Hut and sat outside at a picnic table, shivering slightly from the cold. India's eyes were sparkling across the table at Mick. He was sure now that she really liked him and, while that made him happy, he was becoming aware of an uncomfortable feeling in his stomach, that something wasn't quite right.

As they moved off to look at the display halls, India

started to talk about the Culture Club, and he realised what it was that bothered him.

'It's great that you joined the club,' India said softly, taking his hand this time. 'You know I really had you down as a macho-yobbo type. I used to watch you swaggering round the school with your footy mates and I figured you were just the kind of guys who'd kick sand in the faces of the weaker kids, but then I saw you explaining the set to those year eight boys last week. It was really sweet.'

Mick cringed at the word 'sweet' and, seeing this, India laughed. 'Yes, it was sweet,' she teased. 'But I think that's what being a good leader is all about: helping others understand what's right and wrong and good and bad. I used to think football was stupid, but I guess it can develop leadership qualities. If you weren't so popular through football, maybe you never would have had the courage to join the Culture Club in the first place, when there weren't any other guys in it. I reckon that was really brave.'

Mick felt his heart sink. That was it, then. They seemed to get along so well now, but it was only because

India thought he was someone he wasn't. It took the edge off the evening, and although he tried to be light and friendly, he couldn't quite enjoy himself any more. He kept thinking about Tim Vanda and the way he had treated him. That was just the type of behaviour India would despise. She'd probably even think Tim was a great guy with all the right values if she got to know him.

By the time they were back on the tram, India was well aware that something was wrong. She thought maybe she'd embarrassed Mick by showing she was interested in him, though that didn't seem to fit in with his confident personality.

'What's the matter, Mick?' she asked. 'You seem so quiet. Do you feel sick or something?'

He decided he might as well tell her. Maybe she would understand after all and they'd be able to keep going out together – he hoped so, anyway. And so Mick began the saga of Tim Vanda and how the principal forced him to join the Culture Club. When he'd finished it was time to get off the tram.

They walked in awful silence together to India's

house. In the semi-darkness Mick couldn't really tell what her expression was. He didn't know if she hoped he would kiss her goodnight or if she hoped she never saw him again, so he unlocked his bike and picked up his helmet, then waited a moment before saying, 'So what are the chances you'll go out with me again?'

'None,' snapped India, and turned and walked into the house without a backward glance.

Mick strapped on his helmet and started his ride home. Once he would have thought that she was a stupid twit whose opinion didn't matter. After all, although he had been mean to Tim he had paid for it, hadn't he? Even so, quite often lately he remembered Mrs Vanda's face as she took Tim away from St Andrews.

India, who'd only just come to respect him, now despised him. Maybe it was what he deserved.

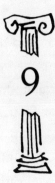

Mick and Jason were sitting together at the front of the bus, both feeling a little sorry for themselves because Rostrevor had just thrashed them by nine goals in the last game of the year. Losing today meant that St Andrews would be officially listed as seventh. It was a small reward for all their time and effort.

'Heard you and the Culture Club are putting on some show tomorrow for next year's parents,' said Jason.

'Could be,' replied Mick. Tomorrow marked the end of Bartel's blackmail. He knew he ought to be happy about being released from the Culture Club, yet he wasn't happy at all.

'Also heard you and India Seidel are the main organisers.'

'Could be.'

'And that you've got the hots for her.'

He was tempted to laugh and say Jason had got it the wrong way around, that *she* was the keen one. Jason probably thought India was dreadful, as no doubt the rest of the team did. But something stopped Mick from lying. To deny his feelings for India would be like denying a part of himself, and he didn't want to do that, not any more.

'Could be,' he said, staring straight ahead.

'Yeah, I reckon she's a bit of all right,' said Jason.

Mick looked sideways at his team mate, not sure if he was joking. 'I thought you'd ...'

'Well, she's unusual, that's for sure. But once you get talking she's great. You taking her out?'

'Thursday night, but I blew it.'

'Same as me when I went out with her.'

'With India?' asked Mick, shocked.

'Don't look so surprised. I'm not just a pretty face and a brilliant footballer. I've got my intellectual side as well.'

'I knew that, Jase,' said Mick, trying not to smile.

Before India Seidel, Mick had gone out with four girls and he'd always been the one to drop them. Michelle Limoux in last term, for instance.

Michelle had been good-looking all right, but she only lasted one date. To begin with, it had proved almost impossible getting any conversation out of her. And when he went to buy the tickets for the movie she made absolutely no attempt to pay. The same thing happened when he bought potato chips and popcorn, and again with the drinks afterwards. Mick was generous with money, so in a way he hadn't minded shouting. What annoyed him was that she just expected it.

They had a pretty hot session at the end of the night

outside her front gate. He enjoyed every second of it, of course, but the whole time he had the strangest feeling Michelle thought it was her way of paying him for the night out. Why this should bother him so much, he wasn't sure. But the fact was, it did.

On Monday morning when they were both in the library working on science projects he wrote a brief note – 'I wish to terminate this relationship' – and slipped it to her.

He had thought it a clever, even humorous, way to call things off. Michelle obviously didn't agree, because she immediately started crying, a little unfortunate considering they were in a quiet library. After a few minutes of this she got up and ran out the door. Reluctantly he followed.

'How could you?' she had cried, when he caught up with her. 'What a cruel way to drop someone.'

He put his hands on her shoulders. 'I'm sorry. I was just trying to make it, you know, funny.'

She sniffed and tried to catch her breath. 'Big joke, Mick. Big bloody joke.'

'All right, I could have put it better.'

She pushed him away from her. 'You're a bastard doing this,' she fumed.

'Come on, Michelle, it's not as if we love each other or anything,' he said, trying to calm the situation.

It clearly didn't work, because she started sobbing worse than she had in the first place, and raced away across the yard. This time he let her go.

What he should have understood by then was that nobody takes rejection very well. It's liable to make a person behave in any number of crazy ways: like Michelle crying loudly in the library when everyone else was silently copying out notes.

Or like Mick deciding to visit an ex-friend for the first time in years.

Still in his blazer and tie from the Rostrevor match, he went there without even going home. Mrs Vanda answered the bell. She narrowed her eyes and kept the screen door shut, as if Mick were there to burgle the place. It took ages to convince her he'd not come to harm Tim. Finally she relented and followed him to a bedroom door at the end of the passage.

'Tim!' she called out. 'Michael Sparrow's here to see

you. Is that all right?'

There was silence for a moment. 'Sure,' came the eventual reply.

Mrs Vanda turned to Mick. 'He's on medication right now, so make sure you don't say anything to upset him,' she warned in a low voice.

He nodded and slid the door open.

'G'day,' said Tim quietly, looking up from his electronic chess game.

'Yeah, g'day,' said Mick.

'Haven't seen you round here for a while.'

'No,' replied Mick, not sure what to say next.

In his discomfort Mick gazed about the room. On one wall was a large, colour photograph showing two young kids hanging by their hands from a gum tree. When Mick recognised himself in it, a terrible thought occurred to him. Tim had kept that picture up there despite all those bad moments between them.

Tim made another move on his chessboard while Mick kept looking around the room. A second photo caught his eye. It was of a short, skinny boy standing proudly in a Camden Primary School footy uniform.

If Camden hadn't been such a small school Tim would never have got that guernsey.

Mick recalled the grand final in their last year there. He had two memories of Tim from that game. Mick remembered him fumbling about with the ball in the goal square when no one was closer than twenty metres, and in the end not even managing to get boot to ball.

Nor could he forget Tim saying that winning wasn't everything as Mick lay on the oval, completely exhausted and trying not to cry, while the Glandore Primary School A's did a lap of honour holding aloft the premiership trophy.

That was the trouble with Timothy Vanda – he had no sense of what was important and what wasn't, so he could really rub people the wrong way. All through their later years at primary school, Mick had protected him from other kids. When they said Tim was the teacher's pet and called him filthy names, Mick went to his rescue. And when no one would sit next to him in class, Mick did.

It wasn't true, though, to say their friendship was

all a one-way street. Tim was weird and didn't know how to get on with ordinary kids, but he was also funny and even interesting in his own strange way. He seemed to know everything about everything and there were lots of times, like peering through his brand new telescope, when Mick had enjoyed his company. It never concerned Mick that they were the only two kids from Camden Primary going to St Andrews – at least not until he got there.

From day one Tim was a dead weight dragging him down. It wasn't like Camden, where Mick had a big enough reputation to not only look after himself but also carry someone else. As other kids formed groups, Mick increasingly found himself sitting alone with Tim at recess and lunch. It was hell. Only when football training began, and Tim joined the table tennis team, did things start falling into place.

Mick began making friends and tasting a bit of popularity. Soon he was not only avoiding Tim but attacking him, proving to himself and to the whole world that Michael Raymond Sparrow was normal.

Tim looked up from his chess. 'I've got no idea why

you're here,' he said, carefully studying the face of his former friend. 'Well, maybe I do.' He sighed and rubbed both hands across his face. 'I get tired a lot. It's this stuff they give me. There are days when I've got more drugs in me than a regular junkie,' he said, smiling.

'Yeah?' said Mick, attempting to smile back. He felt awful. Hurting this guy had been like attacking a defenceless animal.

Tim glanced back down at his chess game. 'If it makes any difference, it wasn't all your fault. I've got to take responsibility for my own life. I realise that now. And I'm even glad to be shifting schools. Going somewhere new means I can leave my mistakes behind, or some of them anyway. I'm going to give it a real go at Glynburn next term. So you're off the hook, Mick, if that's what you want to hear.'

Mick sensed a great heaviness lifting from his shoulders. 'Thanks, Tim. Thanks a lot.'

'Now, if it's all right, I have to start getting ready in a second. We're having dinner with my grandparents.'

'Sure, sure. I just … Look, we've got this spare ticket

for the Crows game next week. Dad bought it for Uncle Matt, but he's going to be away because – '

'Mick,' interrupted Tim.

'Yeah, mate?'

'No need to come around again. Fair enough?'

'Fair enough,' said Mick.

He turned to walk out, but stopped at the doorway. Tim had made it easy for him, but he couldn't leave without saying what he'd come to say.

'I'm sorry I was such a bastard. I guess I was just trying to make myself look good. I never thought about how you'd feel. It was a dumb thing to do.'

Tim nodded.

'Good luck at your new school,' Mick added, then left.

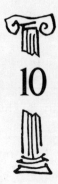

India sat alone on a bench in the quietest quadrangle of the school, not eating her lunch and not waiting for Vanessa to return from the canteen. It was an overcast, dismal day, and it matched her mood. About the only thing she was grateful for was having a few precious minutes by herself. If Vanessa would stop going on about how great the concert for parents went last night and how wonderful the school social was going to be, she might just be bearable company.

Within minutes Vanessa was back, sitting down with a bounce on the bench.

'That was quick,' muttered India, not taking her eyes from the small grey-and-white stone at her feet.

'Didn't go to the canteen,' said Vanessa smugly. 'I ran into Mick and Jason.'

'Oh, yeah,' drawled India, as if totally uninterested. But she looked up anyway. Her friend's face was so sunny the glare hurt her eyes. She looked back at the pebble.

'I've got the best news! Jason's asked me to the social!'

'And you're going with him?'

'I should say so.'

'Great,' India said sarcastically.

'I thought you'd be pleased for me. You *are* my best friend, aren't you?'

'Sorry, Ness. Of course I'm pleased for you.'

'So what's the matter? You're not worried about having to go without me, are you? You know stacks of people. It's not as if you'll be stuck on your own.'

'Oh, no, that doesn't matter. I wasn't going to go, anyway.'

'God, you're a pain these days!' Vanessa exclaimed angrily. 'I just don't know what's the matter with you. Are you waiting for Mick to ask you to the social – is that it?'

'No!' squeaked India, her voice rising with indignation.

'You wouldn't make a good pair,' continued Vanessa. 'He's about as miserable-looking as you are these days. Just when I thought you guys were starting to get on well and you were forgetting all that juvenile stuff about hating footballers.'

'Look,' said India, her eyes flaming. 'I'm glad you're going out with Jason and maybe he's a great guy when you get to know him. I shouldn't say *all* footballers are mindless, but when it comes to Mick ... I know things about him that show he's a two-faced slimeball and a vicious bully too. Did you know he drove Tim Vanda from the school with his steady harassment over the last three years? He ruined the guy's life! That's why Mick Sparrow had to join the Culture Club. Might as well change his name to Hawk, he's so good at swooping on weaker prey. But then isn't that a quality valued on the footy field?'

'Had to join the Culture Club?' queried Vanessa. 'I don't get it.'

India sighed. 'Bartel made him. It was either that or get chucked off the footy team.'

'That's a funny sort of punishment,' said Vanessa. 'So how come you know about this?'

'Mick told me.'

'He told you? You mean he was bragging about it?'

'No, he wasn't bragging,' India replied, recalling the conversation on the tram. 'Actually he sounded pretty upset.'

'Well that's something,' said Vanessa.

'What is?'

'That he cared enough about your opinion to want to set you straight. He may have behaved like a bully, Indy, but you've got to admit it would have taken guts to confess. Especially to someone like you, with all your standards!'

'Mmmm.' India considered this for a moment.

'Maybe.'

'Maybe! What do you mean, maybe? And I suppose you gave him heaps after he told you, and now he's walking round with a face like he's lost the grand final. We all make mistakes, India – it's the decent person who can admit it and feel bad about what they've done.'

India thought about this. She thought about little else for the rest of the afternoon.

Mick stood and looked at his locker for so long nearly everyone else had gone by the time he'd decided which books to put in his bag. He was thinking about the talk he'd just had with Ms Tsouris after English. She'd asked him if he was going to be in Culture Club next term, and he'd had to say no.

It wasn't as if he didn't want to be in it any more, it was just that India would make it too unpleasant to ever be involved with the club again. That was a pity, because he'd really started to enjoy himself, and the amazing thing was, none of his mates had given him a hard time over it. The only person who'd done that was India!

Someone was standing behind him, he realised, waiting to get to their locker.

'Just a moment,' Mick muttered, cramming his thick science book into his bag and slamming his locker door.

He was surprised to see India standing there. Her hair was falling across her shoulders, and there was a determined gleam in her eyes.

'I just wanted you to know that I'm not double dating with you at the social.'

'What?' said Mick, wondering what the hell she was talking about.

'I think Jason and Vanessa should go on their own.'

'Yeah, they are going on their own.'

'Good.'

'I don't mean to be rude, but I didn't ask you to the social.'

'So you don't want to go with me?' she replied, looking down.

'I didn't say that,' replied Mick, wondering how he

had managed to offend her again.

'I suppose you were thinking more of the movies. They're a bit more private.'

'The movies?' Mick felt his blood pressure rise. Did India want to go out with him on another secret date? 'Listen, I don't go on dates in the dark with girls who are too embarrassed to be seen with me in public.'

'So it's the social or nothing?'

'Yes,' he snapped, without thinking.

'Great,' replied India, with a big grin. 'See you Friday night. My stepfather will take us, so make sure you're ready on time!'

Mick laughed as she bounded off down the corridor. The football season might be over, but he now had an even bigger challenge to look forward to.

The Authors

Daryl McCann made a very successful debut as a writer for teenagers with his novel *Street of Dreams* (1992), which is used as a class set in high schools and is now in its third printing. A teacher for many years, he has wide experience of teenagers and writes of their lives and concerns with knowledge and understanding. Daryl was born and educated in Adelaide, and is now a teacher of English at an Adelaide secondary school.

Debbie Forbes has been married to Daryl McCann since 1985, and they have two children. Born in England, Debbie came to Australia in 1962 and has worked in many different fields, including nursing, teaching, market research, retailing, and the hospitality and computer industries. *Culture Shock* is the first book on which she and Daryl have collaborated.

ANOTHER OMNIBUS SHORT

Roadie

David Metzenthen

For Josh, being the road crew for the best undiscovered rock-and-roll band in Melbourne means more than checking the mikes, even if his half-brother is the lead singer. It means trying to get the band their first big break, maybe even a recording contract.

Stranger things have happened – and the night before Crippled Octopus plays at the Jungle Room, Josh knows they are red hot.

An upbeat story (with a serious side) about life in the music business.

ANOTHER OMNIBUS SHORT

Big Night Out

Judith Clarke

Moz, Guster and Davo are treating themselves to a Big Night Out at their favourite venue, the Electric Chair. They've organised a mate to cover for them if their parents ask awkward questions, they've got the right clothes, and just about enough money to swing it.

What could possibly go wrong?

Everything.

An uproariously funny story from the author of the 'Al Capsella' books.

ANOTHER OMNIBUS SHORT

Graffiti Dog

Eleanor Nilsson

Derek is a loner who doesn't always fit in. He's just joined Charlie, Brett and Shaun in the A3 graffiti gang, for something to do. Looking for trouble, his mum says. But then he makes friends with the dog, and he knows instinctively he must keep it a secret from the gang.

Graffiti Dog is a memorable story that shows how a misfit teenage boy finally discovers where he belongs.